Seashore
Wildlife

Includes:

Seashore Biomes

Habitats and Habits

Bird Activities

Mammal Activities

Reptile & Amphibian Activities

Invertebrate Activities

Wildlife Respect

Waterford Press
www.waterfordpress.com

Introduction

There are four main seashore biomes—the coastal marine biome, the ocean marine biome, the rocky shore biome and the sandy shore biome. A biome is a large region that has similar plants, animals and organisms that have adapted to the geography and climate of that area. A biome can have several ecosystems.

An ecosystem is a community of organisms that interact with each other and with their environment. Several ecosystems can exist within a biome. Ecosystems within the world's major seashore biomes include coral reefs, kelp forests, river estuaries, sea grass meadows and salt marshes, as well as rocky cliffs and platforms or sandy beaches.

A wide range of plants and animal species inhabit the ecosystems within these seashore biomes, including whales, sharks, sea turtles, dolphins, crabs, sea stars, seagulls and many others.

Seashore Biomes

Coastal Marine

The part of the ocean you can see from the shore is the coastal marine biome. It reaches from the water line on shore to the continental shelf, where the earth drops away and the ocean suddenly gets much deeper. This biome is found on every continent in the world because it occurs where the land and ocean meet. Fish, crustaceans, whales and other ocean animals often give birth to their young near coastlines where sea grass, kelp or mangroves help hide them from predators.

Ocean Marine

Much of the open ocean is over two miles deep. Sunlight only reaches the top layers of this biome, and the rest of the ocean is in darkness. Since plants need sunlight to live, they do not grow in the deepest part of the ocean, and many of the animals living there drift around without ever touching a firm surface. Some species of jellyfish and octopus inhabit deeper waters.

Sandy Shore

The sandy shore is made up of sand, gravel and shells. These beaches form from sediment that has been carried and deposited by currents and waves. Sandy beaches are found in the US along the coasts of the Atlantic Ocean and Gulf of Mexico. Crustaceans, mollusks, worms and insects all live in sandy shore biomes. Sea birds feed along the waters, and some turtles use the sand for nesting sites.

Rocky Shore

The rocky shore biome features rocky platforms, cliffs, rock pools and boulder fields. These beaches form when soft rocks are worn away by waves and leave harder rocks behind. Rocky shores are found along the western coast of the US but also along New England's shores. Sea urchins, sea stars, mussels, crabs and limpets all live in or on rocky shores. Sea otters live near shore, and the black oystercatcher forages along the shoreline.

Class Act

There are five classes of animals with backbones (vertebrates)
that live in seashore regions.

Draw a line between the animal and the class it belongs to.

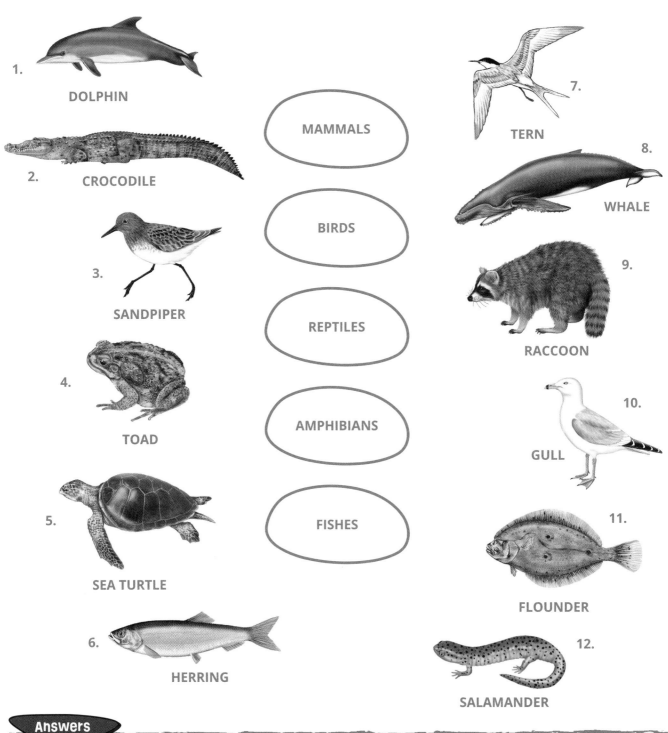

1. DOLPHIN

2. CROCODILE

3. SANDPIPER

4. TOAD

5. SEA TURTLE

6. HERRING

MAMMALS

BIRDS

REPTILES

AMPHIBIANS

FISHES

7. TERN

8. WHALE

9. RACCOON

10. GULL

11. FLOUNDER

12. SALAMANDER

You Are What You Eat

Herbivores eat mostly plants.
Carnivores eat mostly animals.
Omnivores eat plants and animals.

Draw a line between the seashore animal and its diet.

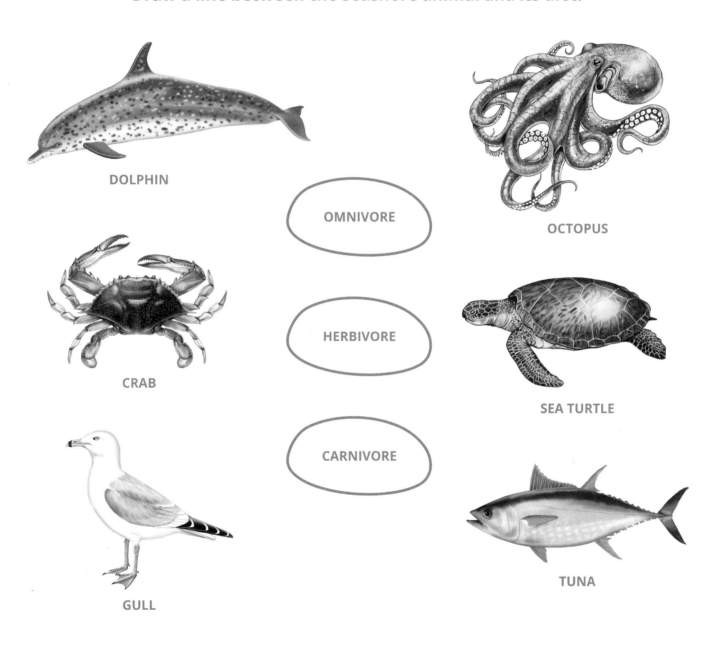

DOLPHIN

OMNIVORE

OCTOPUS

CRAB

HERBIVORE

SEA TURTLE

CARNIVORE

GULL

TUNA

Food Chain

A food chain is the order in which animals feed on other plants and animals. All living things need each other. For instance, a simple food chain might be: crab to jellyfish to sea turtle.

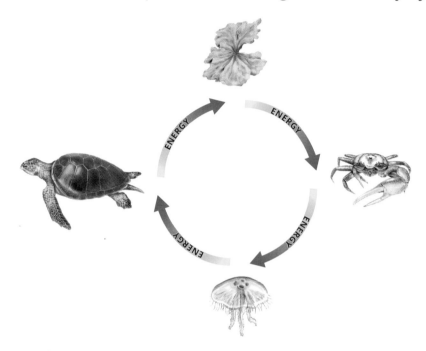

Producers – A producer takes the sun's energy and stores it as food.

Consumers – A consumer feeds on other living things to get energy. Consumers can include herbivores, carnivores and omnivores.

Decomposers – A decomposer consumes waste and dead organisms for energy.

Label each living organism below as a producer, consumer or decomposer.

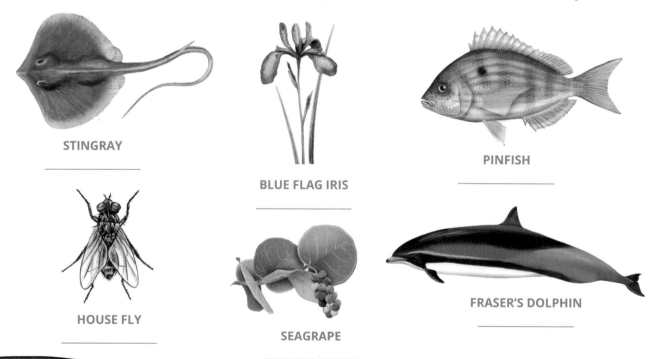

STINGRAY
_____

BLUE FLAG IRIS
_____

PINFISH
_____

HOUSE FLY
_____

SEAGRAPE
_____

FRASER'S DOLPHIN
_____

Find My Home

A habitat provides the things an animal needs for survival: food, shelter, water, the right temperature and protection from predators (animals who prey on other living things).

Draw a line between the animal and its habitat.

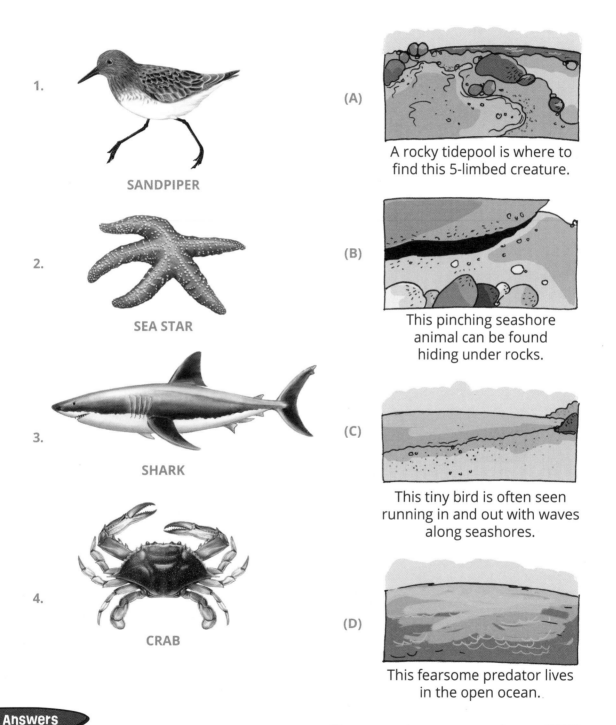

1.

SANDPIPER

2.

SEA STAR

3.

SHARK

4.

CRAB

(A)

A rocky tidepool is where to find this 5-limbed creature.

(B)

This pinching seashore animal can be found hiding under rocks.

(C)

This tiny bird is often seen running in and out with waves along seashores.

(D)

This fearsome predator lives in the open ocean.

Word Search

Coastal marshes are home to hundreds of thousands of wintering geese and ducks. Coastal dunes offer a roosting habitat for wintering shorebirds as well as shelter for other species, like the western snowy plover, that live near coastal waters year-round. Find the names of these nearshore birds in the puzzle.

Find the names of these nearshore birds in the puzzle.

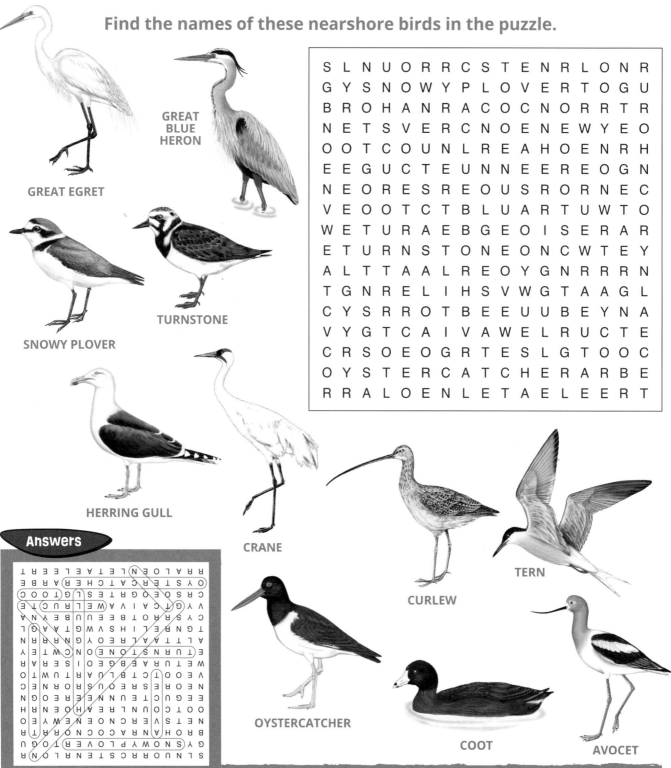

GREAT BLUE HERON

GREAT EGRET

TURNSTONE

SNOWY PLOVER

```
S L N U O R R C S T E N R L O N R
G Y S N O W Y P L O V E R T O G U
B R O H A N R A C O C N O R R T R
N E T S V E R C N O E N E W Y E O
O O T C O U N L R E A H O E N R H
E E G U C T E U N N E E R E O G N
N E O R E S R E O U S R O R N E C
V E O O T C T B L U A R T U W T O
W E T U R A E B G E O I S E R A R
E T U R N S T O N E O N C W T E Y
A L T T A A L R E O Y G N R R R N
T G N R E L I H S V W G T A A G L
C Y S R R O T B E E U U B E Y N A
V Y G T C A I V A W E L R U C T E
C R S O E O G R T E S L G T O O C
O Y S T E R C A T C H E R A R B E
R R A L O E N L E T A E L E E R T
```

HERRING GULL

CRANE

TERN

CURLEW

OYSTERCATCHER

COOT

AVOCET

Name Scramble

Unscramble the letters to form the names
of these familiar seashore creatures.

1.

TOESATRE

2.

CBRA

3.

SERTOBL

4.

LEMSSU

5.

LFSHJYILE

6.

LUGL

7.

TAAESSR

8.

UWRSAL

9

Maze

Oystercatchers are beautiful wading birds that are seen along shorelines searching for shellfish, crabs and other invertebrates.

Help this oystercatcher find the oyster.

ENTER

Word Search

Marine mammals are a group of mammals with unique body parts or behaviors that help them thrive in ocean habitats where temperatures, depths, pressure and darkness are extreme. There are 130 identified species of marine mammals living in Earth's oceans.

Find the names of these marine mammals.

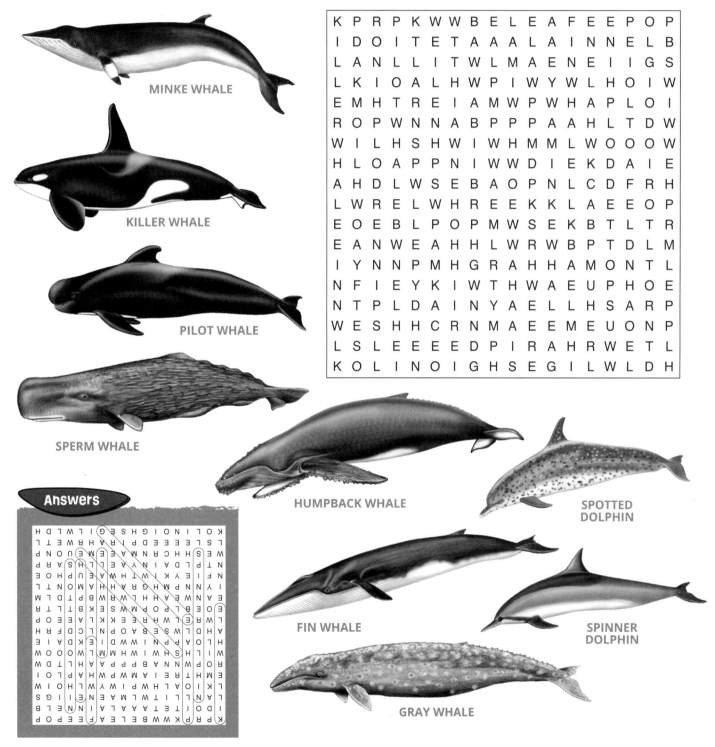

MINKE WHALE

KILLER WHALE

PILOT WHALE

SPERM WHALE

HUMPBACK WHALE

SPOTTED DOLPHIN

FIN WHALE

SPINNER DOLPHIN

GRAY WHALE

```
K P R P K W W B E L E A F E E P O P
I D O I T E T A A A L A I N N E L B
L A N L L I T W L M A E N E I I G S
L K I O A L H W P I W Y W L H O I W
E M H T R E I A M W P W H A P L O I
R O P W N N A B P P P A A H L T D W
W I L H S H W I W H M M L W O O O W
H L O A P P N I W W D I E K D A I E
A H D L W S E B A O P N L C D F R H
L W R E L W H R E E K K L A E E O P
E O E B L P O P M W S E K B T L T R
E A N W E A H H L W R W B P T D L M
I Y N N P M H G R A H H A M O N T L
N F I E Y K I W T H W A E U P H O E
N T P L D A I N Y A E L L H S A R P
W E S H H C R N M A E E M E U O N P
L S L E E E D P I R A H R W E T L
K O L I N O I G H S E G I L W L D H
```

Answers

11

Crossword Puzzle

Animals living in salt marshes must be able to tolerate the saltiness
and changes in water levels brought on by the tides and freshwater that flows in.
Mammals are drawn to the abundant seeds and leaves of the marsh plants.
Many mammals that live here are small, quick and elusive.

Use the clues about salt marsh mammals to help solve the puzzle.

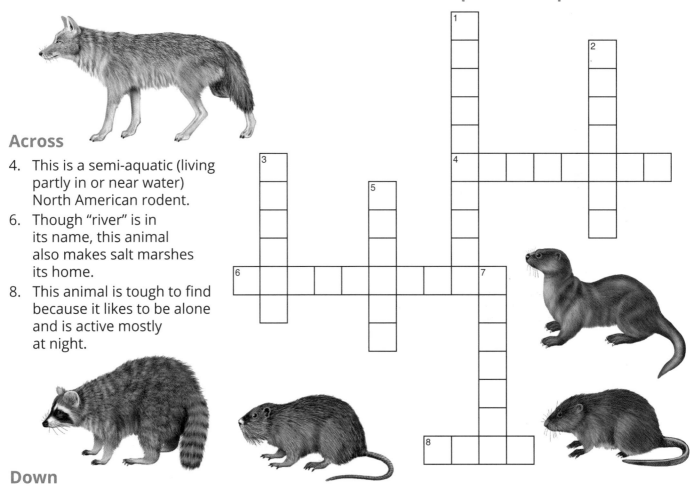

Across

4. This is a semi-aquatic (living partly in or near water) North American rodent.
6. Though "river" is in its name, this animal also makes salt marshes its home.
8. This animal is tough to find because it likes to be alone and is active mostly at night.

Down

1. This endangered species comes to the salt marsh to feed on the plant matter found there.
2. This animal has a long, scaly rudder-like tail that is flattened on both sides.
3. This invasive species was introduced to the United States because of its fur. An invasive species is a living thing that was introduced to a new place where it didn't belong and can cause harm to the environment.
5. This dog-like mammal comes to the salt marsh to hunt the smaller animals that feed there.
7. This animal is an omnivore that visits the salt marsh during low tide to eat crabs, shrimp, fish or anything in its diet.

Answers

Across: 4. Marsh Rat
6. River Otter
8. Mink

Down: 1. Pygmy Mouse
2. Muskrat
3. Nutria

5. Coyote
7. Raccoon

Name Scramble

Unscramble the letters to form the names of these marine mammals.

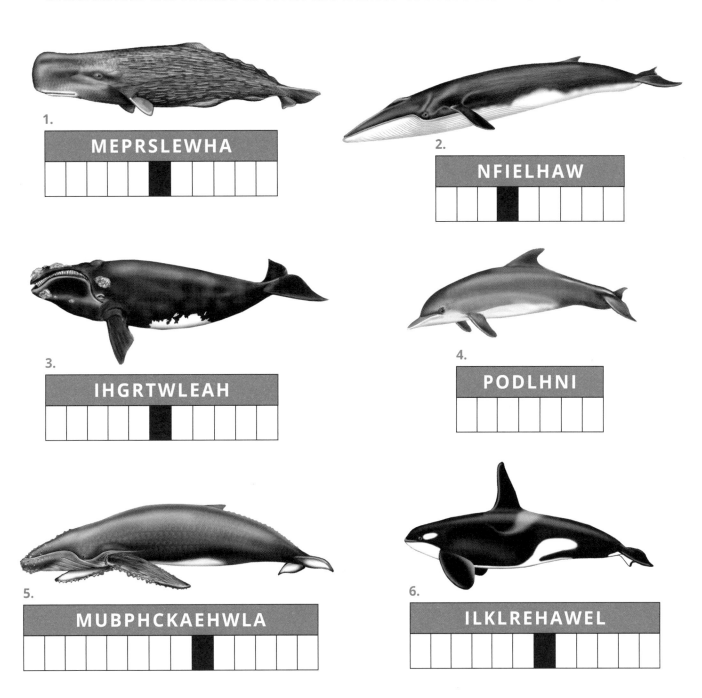

1.
MEPRSLEWHA

2.
NFIELHAW

3.
IHGRTWLEAH

4.
PODLHNI

5.
MUBPHCKAEHWLA

6.
ILKLREHAWEL

Origami

The **Atlantic stingray** is a flat fish that feeds on worms, crabs, shellfish, shrimp and small fish. It is found in the western Atlantic Ocean and the Gulf of Mexico. It has a sharp barb at the base of its tail that can inject poison, but it will not attack unless threatened. To avoid startling a stingray and being stung, shuffle your feet while walking into the surf or shallow waters. This is called the "stingray shuffle."

Starting with a square piece of paper, follow the simple folding instructions below to create a stingray.

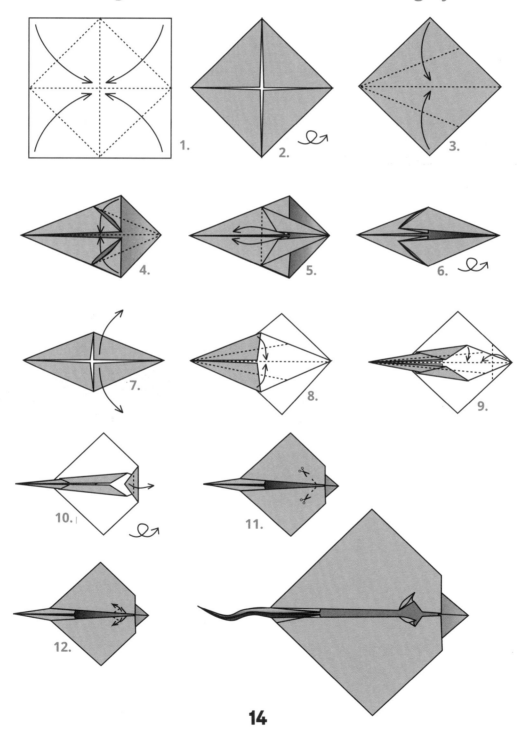

Oddball Out

In each row, circle the animal that is different from the others.

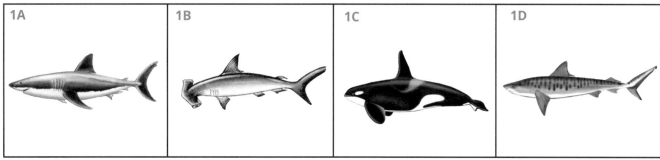

| 1A | 1B | 1C | 1D |

Three of these are sharks; one is not.

| 2A | 2B | 2C | 2D |

Three of these are shells; one is not.

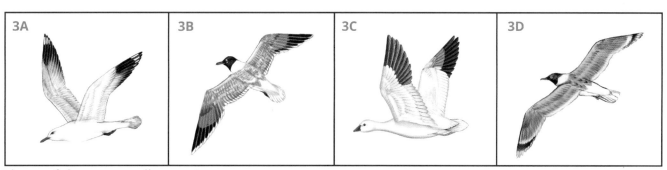

| 3A | 3B | 3C | 3D |

Three of these are gulls; one is not.

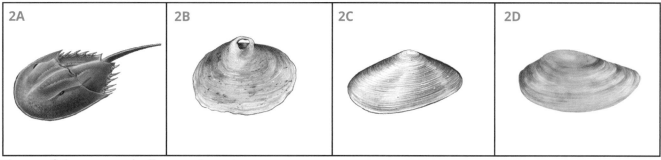

| 4A | 4B | 4C | 4D |

Three of these are salmon; one is not.

Name Scramble

Unscramble the letters to form the names of these familiar fishes.

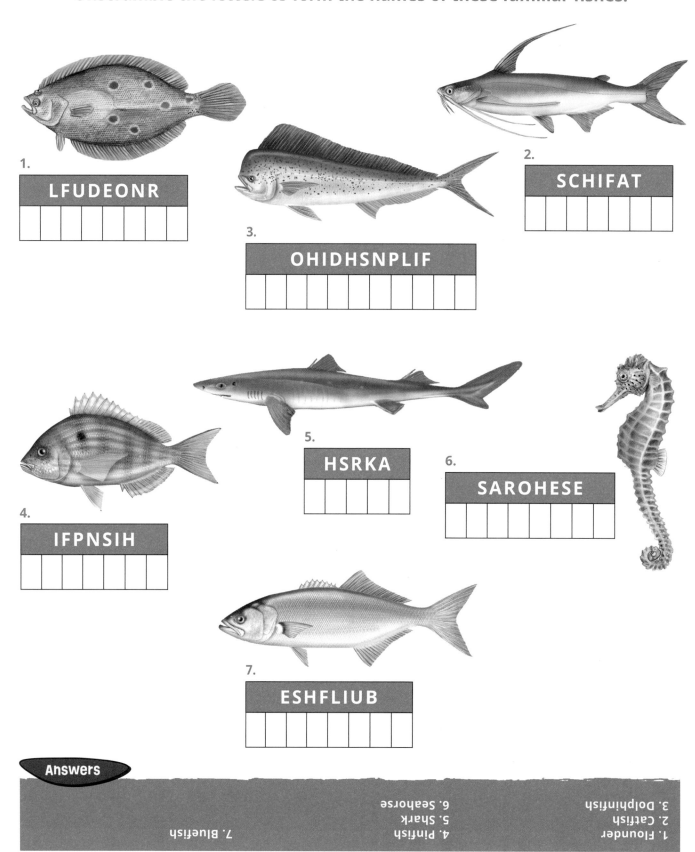

1.

LFUDEONR

2.

SCHIFAT

3.

OHIDHSNPLIF

5.

HSRKA

6.

SAROHESE

4.

IFPNSIH

7.

ESHFLIUB

Make Words

Common in tropical waters, there are at least 114 species of **butterflyfish**. A close cousin of the angelfish, most are brightly colored in shades of yellow, white, black, blue, red and orange. Some have eyespots on their back ends, which helps confuse predators. Butterflyfish spend their time pecking their long snouts into coral and rock formations to hunt for coral polyps, worms and other small invertebrates.

How many words can you make from the letters in butterflyfish?

_____   _____

_____   _____

_____   _____

_____   _____

_____   _____

_____   _____

_____   _____

Maze

The **great barracuda** is a large predatory, ray-finned fish with a long mouth, sharp teeth and very powerful jaws. It is well-built for the hunt. Its silver sides and white belly make it hard to see among reefs in the open Gulf. Due to its large size, the barracuda has very few predators besides dolphins, sharks and Goliath groupers. This fish is an expert hunter but cannot eat a human—though it may charge toward you if you have any shiny objects with you in the water.

Help the great barracuda find its way to the anchovies as quickly as possible!

ENTER

Shadow Know-How

Can you identify these marine mammals?

Name Scramble

Unscramble the names of these familiar fishes.

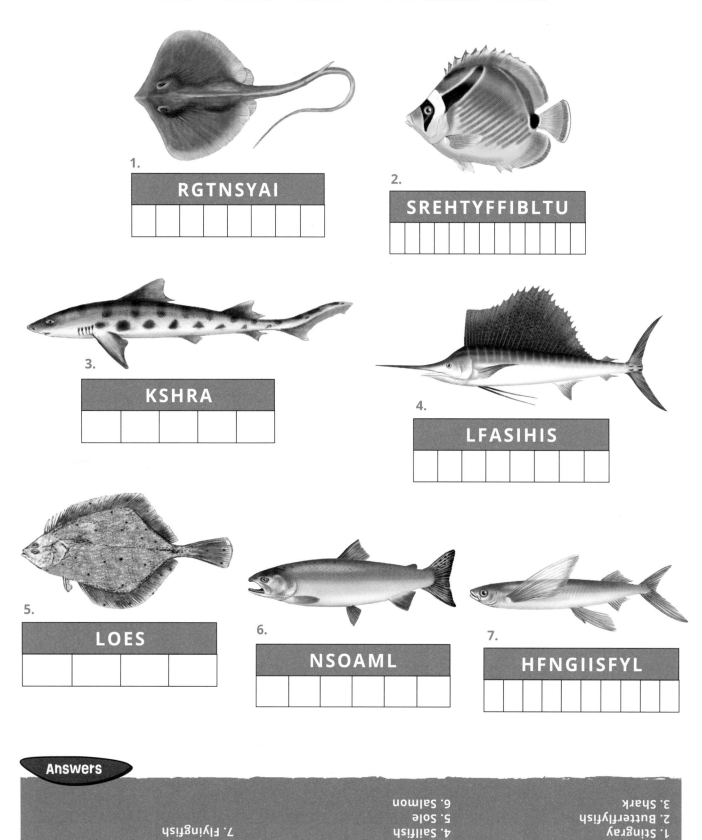

1.

RGTNSYAI

2.

SREHTYFFIBLTU

3.

KSHRA

4.

LFASIHIS

5.

LOES

6.

NSOAML

7.

HFNGIISFYL

Name Match

There are seven species of sea turtles in the world. The five shown below, plus the olive ridley, can be found throughout the ocean. A seventh species, the flatback, is found only in Australia. All of the species are endangered except for the loggerhead, which is classified as threatened. Endangered animals are in danger of becoming extinct. Threatened animals may soon become endangered if nothing is done to help them. Sea turtles only return to land to lay eggs, and most males never return.

Draw a line between the sea turtle and its name.

1.

2.

3.

A. KEMP'S RIDLEY SEA TURTLE

B. HAWKSBILL SEA TURTLE

C. LOGGERHEAD SEA TURTLE

D. LEATHERBACK SEA TURTLE

E. GREEN SEA TURTLE

4.

5.

1. This is the smallest and most endangered sea turtle.
2. This turtle is not named for the color of its shell but for the greenish color of its skin.
3. The most tropical species of sea turtle, it likes to stay near reefs to feed.
4. This is the largest and fastest-growing of all sea turtles. It can grow up to eight feet long and weigh 1300 pounds.
5. This sea turtle is a carnivore with powerful jaws. It feeds mostly on shellfish that live on the bottom of the ocean.

Answers

1. A
2. E
3. B
4. D
5. C

Origami

Starting with a square piece of paper, follow the simple folding instructions below to create a sea turtle.

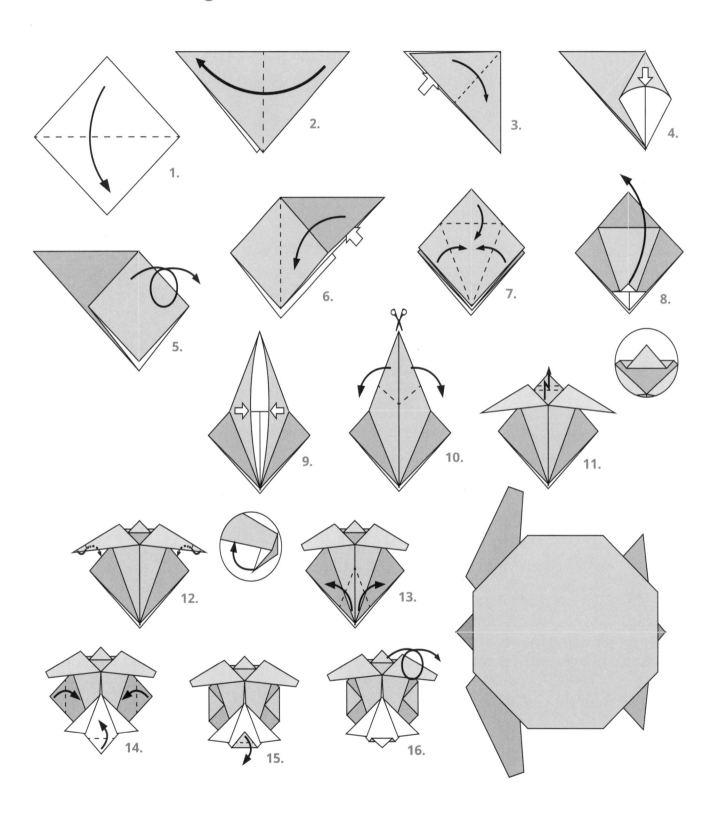

Be An Artist

Copy this loggerhead sea turtle by drawing it one square at a time.

The **loggerhead sea turtle** is the largest of all hard-shelled turtles. It has a large head with strong jaws. Its flippers work like wings in the water to help it stabilize and steer. It is a "keystone" species, which means that other animals in its ecosystem also depend on it for survival. An ecosystem is a community of living organisms that interact with each other and their environment.

Color Key

Make Words

The **American crocodile** is a large reptile found in coastal waters in extreme southern Florida. Although related to the alligator, you can tell the crocodile by its longer, pointier snout. And while alligators like freshwater environments, crocodiles live in both freshwater and saltwater. Alligators and crocodiles live together in only one place on Earth—the Florida Everglades.

How many words can you make from the letters in the American crocodile's name?

_____   _____

_____   _____

_____   _____

_____   _____

_____   _____

_____   _____

_____   _____

Be An Artist

Draw this hermit crab by copying one square at a time.

The **hermit crab** is a small crab that protects itself by living in the shells of sea snails. It is often seen scurrying around on the sand and rocks near the water line. The shell acts like a mobile home. When threatened, it will withdraw all but its hard, protective claws into the shell.

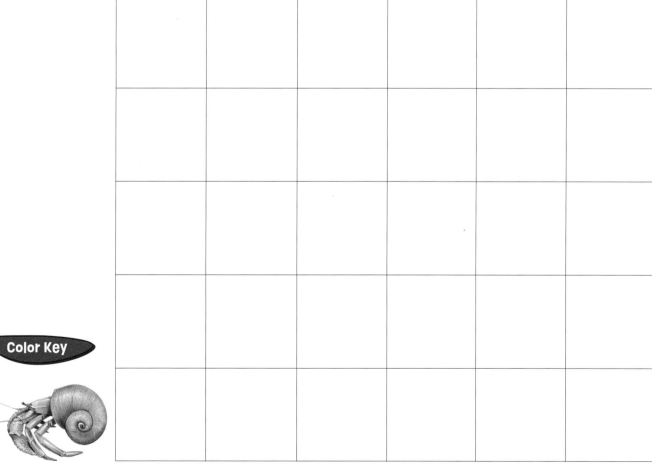

Color Key

Shadow Know-How

Can you identify these birds?

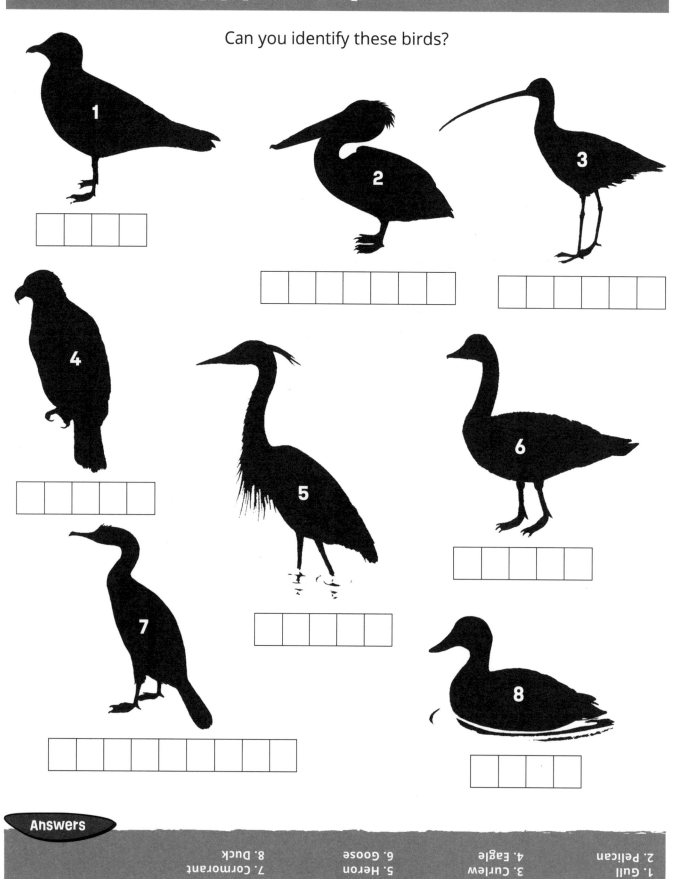

Word Search

These sea creatures have something in common—they are all invertebrates, which means they do not have bones. These animals are an important part of the food web. Not only do they serve as food for birds, fish and mammals, but they also help break down organic matter in the ocean. Most need oxygen to live. Some have small gills. Others have little holes that absorb oxygen that has dissolved in the water. Some use breathing tubes that rise about the water's surface, and others bring air bubbles from the surface down under the water with them.

Find the names of the animals in this puzzle.

COMMON SEA STAR

KEYHOLE URCHIN

WARTY SEA ANEMONE

SEA NETTLE

MANTIS SHRIMP

D	U	B	I	Y	A	I	H	E	M	G	H	A	M	T	I	M	A
J	I	M	Y	H	R	N	L	R	E	H	Y	S	G	E	O	T	S
R	N	I	A	S	A	C	Y	E	I	L	A	P	E	N	S	A	I
A	M	E	E	R	A	T	S	A	E	S	N	O	M	M	O	C	L
E	R	E	J	N	O	S	H	A	E	E	R	M	E	E	A	S	L
K	A	L	R	H	C	I	K	O	C	R	T	H	A	N	H	A	R
E	W	A	R	T	Y	S	E	A	A	N	E	M	O	N	E	N	R
G	B	S	K	E	Y	H	O	L	E	U	R	C	H	I	N	E	U
G	E	E	S	I	T	E	L	T	T	E	N	A	E	S	J	I	A
E	Y	A	H	R	A	T	S	A	E	S	D	E	D	N	A	B	N
K	O	T	S	H	R	N	T	P	N	N	A	E	O	L	H	S	A
E	S	O	T	L	T	E	P	K	C	R	P	A	L	S	F	S	D
A	N	M	L	M	L	N	E	A	S	E	A	W	H	I	P	T	S
K	R	W	L	S	S	S	A	L	E	A	L	A	M	S	Y	Y	N
E	T	S	H	N	E	L	O	A	M	C	R	S	E	W	A	T	A
E	A	S	R	H	S	I	F	Y	L	L	E	J	N	O	O	M	T
R	E	C	A	P	M	I	R	H	S	S	I	T	N	A	M	M	H
E	R	A	T	S	A	E	S	Y	A	R	G	E	R	E	M	R	H

SEA WHIP

MOON JELLYFISH

GRAY SEA STAR

BARNACLE

BANDED SEA STAR

27

Origami

There are about 2,000 species of sea star, all of which live in saltwater. They use tiny tube feet on the underside of their "arms" to move. They also use these tube feet to hold on to objects like rocks when strong waves roll in. Not all sea stars have five arms—some species have as many as 50! These amazing creatures also have the ability to grow new body parts if needed.

Starting with a square piece of paper, follow the simple folding instructions below to create a sea star.

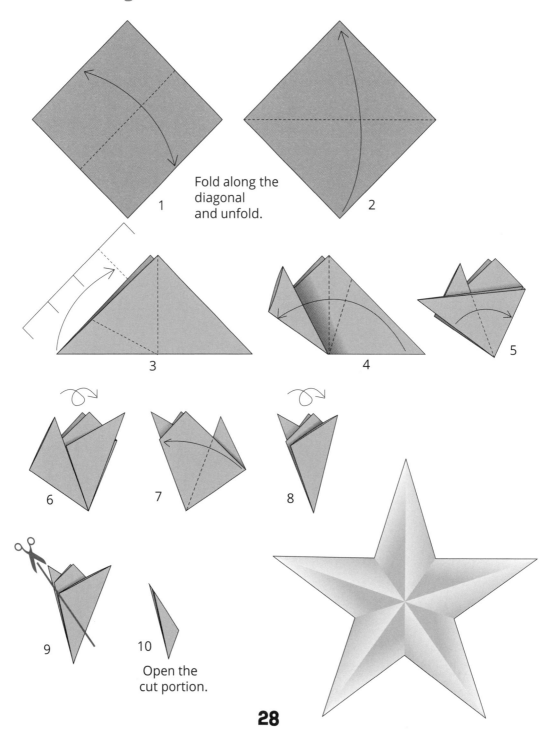

Fold along the diagonal and unfold.

1

2

3

4

5

6

7

8

9

10

Open the cut portion.

Name Match

Draw a line between the marine invertebrate and its name.

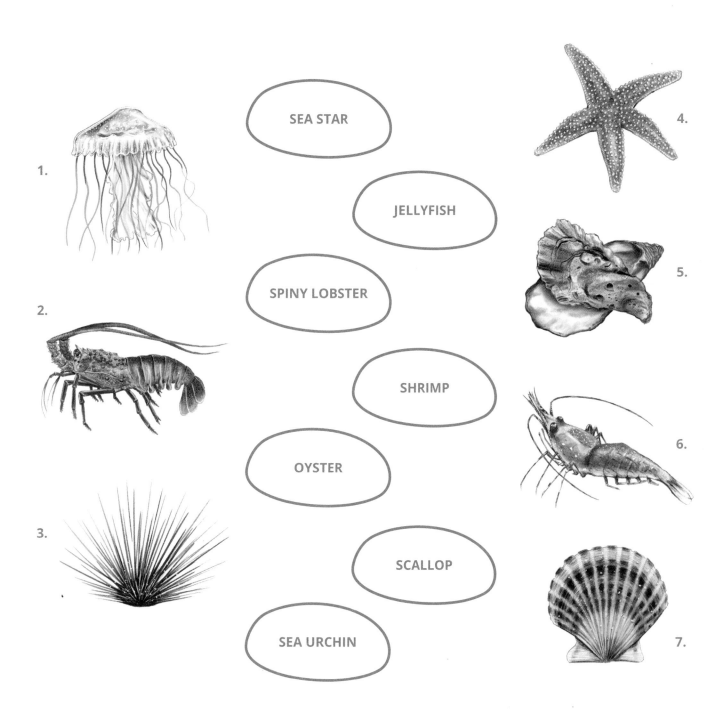

1.

2.

3.

SEA STAR

JELLYFISH

SPINY LOBSTER

SHRIMP

OYSTER

SCALLOP

SEA URCHIN

4.

5.

6.

7.

Connect the Dots

Crustaceans live in freshwater and saltwater. They have hard external skeletons that support and protect their bodies. Shrimps, crabs, lobsters and crayfish are all common crustaceans.

Connect the dots to reveal this familiar seashore crustacean.

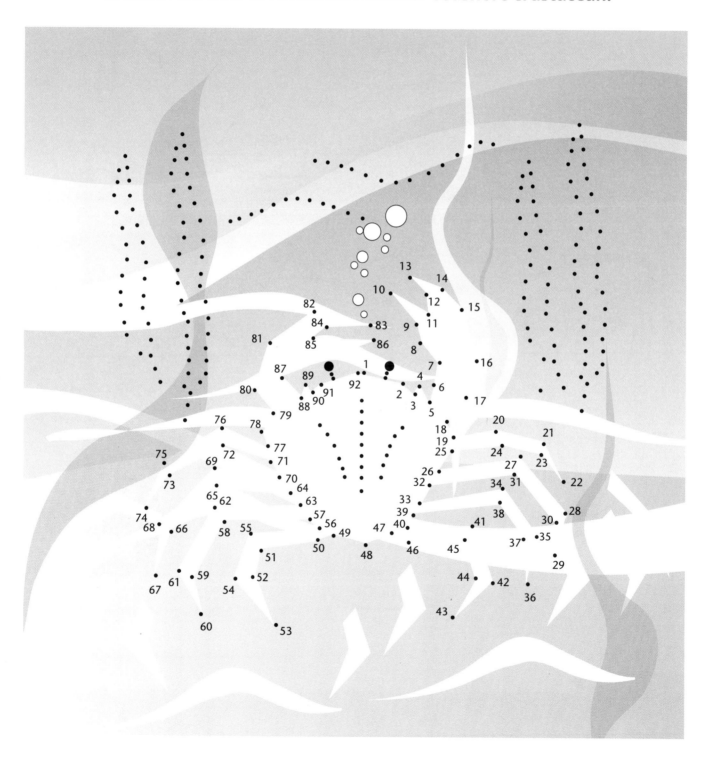

Word Search

Plants that grow in sandy coastal areas can tolerate wind, salt and sand. Some species store saltwater in their leaves between rainy seasons. Many grow low to the ground to avoid wind-blown sand, and others have light-colored leaves to reflect harsh sunlight.

Find the names of these seashore plants in the puzzle.

```
O F E S G E A O N A S C W M L L
V E R L A E W O F L R H D L L T
G R E E R D E O L O D E N O G C
G S A G I A H L L O A G G C H O
L L L O R F E E R A L F N E L D
N H D B D N E N T T V G N E S E
W O L L A M E S O R G I E D E E
R E L G N D E R S B L E B S A W
W C A A L V D L T L G L E C L F
R C V O E A A R E G N L A I A L
D A G W R M S W U E O C C C V U
R T E E E R E S W H D R H E E G
E T H I L E D L W L E D R N N E
R A T F D D B E F O S L O G D D
D I L D A T E E L T R O S H E F
E L G A N B N E A S T T E A R O
```

BEACH ROSE

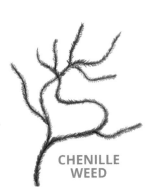

CHENILLE WEED

ROSE MALLOW

GOLDENROD

GULFWEED

CATTAIL

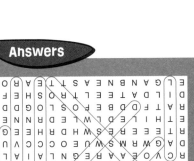
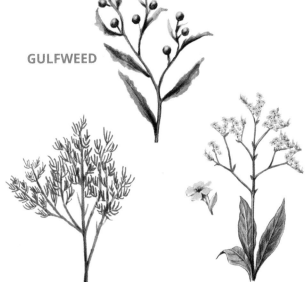

GLASSWORT

SEA LAVENDER

Wildlife Respect

In wild spaces, humans are the visitors. We are lucky to be able to observe animals in their natural habitats. Along with that privilege, comes a responsibility to respect the animals we see, as well as their homes. The best way to learn about wildlife is by quietly watching. Though the possibility of getting a better look—or a better photo—can be tempting, getting too close can be stressful to a wild animal.

Here are some ways you can help reduce the number of disruptive human encounters that wild animals experience:

1. Know the site before you go.

2. When taking photos, do not use a flash, which can disturb animals.

3. Give animals room to move and act naturally.

4. Visit after breakfast and before dinner when wild animals are less active.

5. Do not touch or disturb the animals.

6. Do not feed the animals.

7. Store your food and take your trash with you.

8. Read and respect signs.

9. Do not make quick movements or loud noises.

10. Report any encounters with dangerous animals.